PUFFIN

The Bus Under the Leaves

Adam lived with his parents in a house on the hillside, with fields full of cows all around. He often wished the cows would turn into children he could play with, because he felt lonely on his own. But all that changed when he made friends with their neighbour, old Mr John Miller, and with David, the little boy who came to stay with him.

Adam knew there would be lots of things to do now. He could take David fishing for eels and tree climbing, and they would be able to ride in the blue trolley Mr Miller had made, that was going to have an old car horn and number plates — it was all going to be great, he knew. But the very best thing of all, the one Adam *didn't* know about, was Mr Miller's forgotten secret, the very old bus hidden away among the creepers.

All children enjoy having their own private camp or hide-out, and Margaret Mahy's simple but imaginative story of a summer friendship and a very special den will delight every one of them.

For readers of seven and over.

MARGARET MAHY

The Bus
Under the Leaves

Illustrated by Margery Gill

PUFFIN BOOKS

PUFFIN BOOKS

Penguin Books (N.Z.) Ltd, 182–190 Wairau Road,
Auckland 10, New Zealand

Penguin Books Ltd, 27 Wrights Lane, London W8 5TZ
(Publishing & Editorial)
and Harmondsworth, Middlesex, England (Distribution & Warehouse)

Viking Penguin Inc., 40 West 23rd Street, New York,
New York 10010, U.S.A.

Penguin Books Australia Ltd, Ringwood, Victoria, Australia

Penguin Books Canada Limited, 2801 John Street, Markham,
Ontario, Canada L3R 1B4

First published by J. M. Dent & Sons 1974
Published in Puffin Books 1976
Reprinted 1979
This edition first published 1988
Copyright © Margaret Mahy, 1974

All rights reserved

Printed in Australia by
The Book Printer

I

THERE was once a boy called Adam who lived on a hillside. He did not just live on the hillside like a tree or a gorsebush. He had a house and a mother and father, and even a garden with a potato in it and a bean climbing up a stick.

All around Adam's house and garden were paddocks with cows in them. He liked the cows, but often he wished that they would turn into children he could play with. He got tired of being alone all the time.

The only house nearby belonged to an old man who lived across the road. He was a tall brown old man with a white beard like a famous old explorer. He had a garden full of trees and flowers and vegetables. Adam used to watch him going up and down hoeing and raking.

"That old man is a witch-man," he said to his mother. "Sometimes he turns into a tree."

"He does look like a tree, because he is so tall," his mother said, "but he is not a witch-man. His name is John Miller, and he is very kind."

One day Adam climbed up the hedge. He wriggled up through all the scratchy twigs until his head came out at the top – out into the sunshine and wind again. He could see the hills and the paddocks, which were brown because it was summer and the grass was dry. Below him he could see the road too, covered in dust and stones. As he looked up and down it he suddenly saw a very strange sight. There was Mr John Miller pulling a boy's trolley behind him. It was the biggest trolley Adam had ever seen. It was painted blue, and its wheels made a lovely

6

rattly sound as they went over the bumps. As Adam stared Mr John Miller did a funny thing. He tried to climb into the trolley himself. Of course he was too tall for it, and the trolley tipped over so that Mr John Miller fell into the dust. He got up quickly and looked round to see if anyone had seen him fall out. The first thing he saw was Adam with his head sticking out from the top of the hedge, staring until his eyes stood out like door knobs.

"Hello!" said Mr John Miller. "I am just trying out this trolley."

"You are a bit too big for it," Adam told him.

"It is such a long time since I rode in a trolley, I thought I would like to see if I remembered how to do it," Mr John Miller explained. "But I have forgotten."

"Is it your trolley?" asked Adam.

"I made it," said Mr John Miller, "but not for myself. There is a little boy coming to stay with me."

Adam sat very still in the hedge looking hard at Mr John Miller.

"As little as me?" he asked, "or a lot littler?"

"About as big as you," Mr John Miller replied. "Maybe you should come down and try this trolley. I can't, because it's too small for me."

Quick as a wink Adam climbed out of the hedge, getting a few scratches on the way down. The trolley was the best he had ever seen. When he got into it he felt that it was the sort of trolley a king might get for Christmas. He took hold of the ropes.

"Are you ready?" called Mr John Miller.

"Yes," Adam called back. Mr John Miller gave the trolley a push with his foot and off it went, slowly at first then faster and faster. Adam yelled and Mr John Miller cheered and waved his arms. It was a wonderful ride.

"Well, that's a good thing," Mr John Miller said. "I was afraid the trolley might not be any good. I am glad I met you. Would you like to come to my house to have a drink of ginger-beer and some cake? I made the cake last night."

"My mother makes our cakes," Adam said.

"I have no mother," Mr John Miller said sadly, "so I must make cakes for myself. This cake is rather burnt, but it is nice to eat in a burnt sort of way. I think the oven was too hot. We'll have some ginger-beer too."

They went in at Mr John Miller's gate, pulling the trolley after them. It was cool under the poplar trees and the sunlight came through in little pieces, looking like gold money lying on the grass.

"Suppose the sunshine was gold," said Adam, "we would be rich. We could buy a fire engine."

"I would buy a camel," said Mr John Miller, "and ride it to the shop. I would buy my butter and bread and things and pack them on the camel's back and ride home again."

At the back of Mr John Miller's house was a grassy lawn, and a clothes-line with Mr John Miller's socks on it. Behind the clothes-line was a row of trees and behind the trees was a big pile of boxes, rusty tins, tyres and other lumpy-looking things.

"What is that?" asked Adam.

"It's a dump," said Mr John Miller. "I used to fix cars for people, and those are broken pieces of car. Stay here and I will go and get the cake and ginger-beer. I won't be a moment."

Adam liked the look of the dump. He thought he could find a lot of interesting things there. Over the rusty lumpy pieces a plant with big green leaves was creeping. It climbed over the wall and most of the dump. By the time Adam had looked at this plant Mr John Miller was back. He had a tray in his

hands and on it was a plate of cake slices and two
mugs of ginger-beer. The cake was dark brown and
full of raisins.

When Adam lifted up his mug to drink it began
to play a tune.

"Have you heard of a musical-box?" asked Mr
John Miller. "That is a musical-mug. It plays 'Here
we go round the Mulberry Bush'."

"I thought it was magic," said Adam. "It gave me
a fright."

They sat on the step and ate cake.

Then Mr John Miller said:

"This boy I have coming to stay with me is called David. He has been sick and the doctor said he must come and stay in the country. He lives in the town and has never been in the country before. I think I might be too old to play with him. Would you like to come down and play with him?"

"Yes!" said Adam. "I would like that. Often I wish I had boys to play with. It is all right when I go to school, but in the holidays I feel a bit lonely."

"Will you find plenty to do?" asked Mr John Miller.

"Yes," said Adam. "We will fish for eels and make dams across the creek with stones. Some days we can try catching frogs. I have a good climbing tree at my house too."

"There is the trolley I have made," said Mr John Miller. "I will put a car's number-plate on it, and an old car horn."

Adam's eyes shone. He thought of speeding down the hill, tooting the horn as he went.

12

"When is David coming?" he asked.

"Tomorrow!" said Mr John Miller. "Tomorrow morning I will get him from the station. Would you like to come with me?"

"Yes – I'd like to, a lot," said Adam.

Just then he heard his mother calling him for lunch.

"I'll ask my mother," cried Adam. "I think she will let me come."

"Make sure you don't forget!" said Mr John Miller. "I will walk to the gate with you. Take the last bit of cake. Maybe your mother will be cross with me for filling you up with cake – you won't want any lunch."

"I always want lunch," Adam said quickly.

As he ran back up the hill he thought how nice Mr John Miller was and how silly he had been to think he was a witch-man.

"He is tall and brown like a tree, though," thought Adam. "Perhaps one day he will grow leaves out of his ears and fingers." This idea made him laugh to himself. Then he thought how wonderful it would be to have a boy to play with.

"Two new friends," he said to himself. "Mr John Miller today and David tomorrow. I hope David will like me. This morning I was lonely. Now I am not lonely any more."

He looked at the brown hills and smiled at them because he felt so excited and happy.

2

NEXT morning Adam's mother made him put on clean clothes before he went to Mr John Miller's house.

"Be a good boy!" she said. She always said that.

Mr John Miller was polishing up his car. It was painted blue like the trolley.

"Your car is a funny car," Adam said.

"Is it?" Mr John Miller said, blinking his eyes in a surprised way. "I put it together myself out of pieces of other cars. It is a patchwork car. I call it Blue

Pig because when it goes uphill it grunts like a lazy old pig. Get in and off we go."

When they got to the station the train was just coming round the corner. As it came along it sounded as if it was quarrelling with the railway lines in a cross, chattering voice. This was the railway-train noise. When it stopped two people got out. One was a man who walked away quickly. The other was David. He was not as tall as Adam. His hair was black and it stuck flat on his head. Adam thought that it looked as if it was painted on with black paint. His face was not brown like Adam's face. It was white and thin. He had a little suitcase in his hand.

"You must be David," said Mr John Miller. "I am John Miller and this is Adam Brown."

"Hello," said David.

"The car is over here," Mr John Miller told him. "We will soon be home."

David looked at the Blue Pig as if he did not like it very much. When they were inside the car, he said, "My father has a new car. It is green and has four headlights."

"Mr John Miller made this car himself," Adam told David. "It is hard to make cars too."

"Our car is a lot longer than this one," David said.

He did not sound shy, but he did not sound friendly either. As they drove through the country to Mr John Miller's house Adam showed David Mr Jones's cows and where you could find mushrooms. David did not say anything for a long time.

Then he said, "Where are the shops?"

"There aren't any shops," said Mr John Miller. "There are nothing but farms in the country."

"Where do you get your bread?" asked David. His eyes were round as pennies with surprise.

"It comes in a van," Adam said. "We ring up the grocer and tell him what we want. Then he drives out here and brings it in to us."

David looked worried and grew quiet again. They reached Mr John Miller's house.

"Don't bother to unpack your things now," Mr John Miller said to David. "Adam will show you round the garden while I get you something to eat."

He went into the house and took David's suitcase with him.

"What a funny man," David whispered to Adam. "Why doesn't he get his beard cut off?" Adam felt very angry.

"He is a kind sort of man," he replied, "and he can make good cakes. He'll give us cake and ginger-beer in a minute."

"He's all right," said David. "But he is still funny. I didn't really want to stay with him. I wanted to go with my brother to the Scout Camp. They cook sausages over a fire and have lots of fun. I am too small to go."

Adam felt more angry with David than ever. He had wanted another boy to play with so much, but now that David was here he was not friendly.

Adam wanted to go home but he felt it would not be fair to Mr John Miller. Instead he said, "Come and look at Mr John Miller's dump. There are pieces of cars in it – old engines, all rusty! Some tyres too." David followed him slowly. They climbed up on to the pile of rusty iron. As they went they crushed the green creeping plant with their shoes. There was not much to see.

"Over the wall is the creek," Adam said. "I can swim a bit – I learned to swim when I was five." He climbed onto something hard and lumpy covered all over with creeper. "If you climb up beside me you can see the creek."

David looked up at him and nodded his head. He did not even try to climb up by Adam. Adam did not know what to say next. He began to kick at the creeper. He pushed at it with his foot. Under the leaves some glass appeared.

"Hey!" said Adam. "There's a window here under this plant."

David stared. This time he did come up beside Adam, looking interested at last. They pulled at the creeper with their hands and more glass showed under it. It really was a window – a window that had been hidden away behind the green leaves. It was very dirty, but when they pressed their noses against it and stared through they could see a steering

wheel and a driver's seat. Behind that were more
seats.

"Do you know what?" David cried. "This is a
bus – a truly bus all covered over by the creeper.
This is the front window – the windscreen. Here, by
my hand, is a windscreen wiper. We are standing on
its bonnet. Let's pull the creeper off it."

"We must ask Mr John Miller," said Adam.

At that moment Mr John Miller himself appeared, carrying a tray with plates on it. There were scones and little cakes, and mugs of ginger-beer as well.

"Mr John Miller," Adam called, "we have found a bus in your dump. How did it get here?"

"Well, think of that!" said Mr John Miller. "I had forgotten it. I bought it years ago and put its engine and wheels onto another bus. The creeper has covered it, but you can pull it off if you like."

Adam saw David's turned-down mouth suddenly turn up at the corners and he smiled all over his face. Adam had never seen such a wide smile. He forgot he was angry with David.

"We can pull the creeper off and make a fort," David cried. "We'll have good fun. We'll eat the cakes first though."

After they had eaten the scones and little cakes, and drunk every drop of ginger-beer, David and Adam began to pull the creeper off the old bus.

It was hard work for there was a lot of creeper and

sometimes it was very thick. As they pulled it off, the bus began to show – first the windscreen and bonnet, and then a long row of windows along one side. The windows looked like worried little square eyes peering out from under untidy green hair. The bus was not as tall as most buses because its wheels were gone.

Once it had been painted red. Now it had faded to pink, not a pretty pink, but a dirty pink. In some places there were big patches of rust.

"Open the door," David said. "Let's go in." But the door would not open.

"Mr Miller!" called Adam. "This bus has a door to go in by, but we can't get it open."

"Well, I can soon fix that," said Mr Miller.

He came along with a big red oil can, some sandpaper, a screwdriver and a hammer. He oiled the hinges and unscrewed the lock. He scraped rust off with the sandpaper, and cleared dirt and dead leaves out from all round the door. He hooked the claw end of the hammer round the edge of the door and pulled. The door came open. The boys and Mr John Miller went into the bus.

Inside it was dark and dirty. The floor was coming to pieces. The seats looked sad and empty without any people in them.

"We'll have to fix it up for you," Mr John Miller said. "I'll see what I can do. First I must take out most of those seats. You boys pull the creeper down outside while I clean it up a bit inside."

The boys worked outside the bus and Mr John Miller worked inside. He banged with a hammer and sawed with a saw. Out came some of the dirty old seats. Out came pieces of rotten floor.

"Let's leave the creeper on the roof," David said to Adam. "It will look like a jungle house then."

All afternoon they worked hard clearing out the bus. Then Adam's mother came down to find him. The creeper was cleared away from the sides of the bus. David and Adam had a bucket of soapy water and were washing the windows. Mr John Miller had put half a new floor in the bus. Only four of the old seats were left – two at the front and two at the back. Adam's mother said, "Goodness, you are busy!"

"Look!" Adam said. "Look at the bus! Me and David are going to make a fort out of it."

Adam's mother said, "You must come home now, Adam. Tomorrow you can come and play with David again."

"Oh yes," David said, "Mr John Miller and I need someone to help us build a fort."

"I'll have some work for Adam tomorrow," said Mr John Miller. "There is too much work for just David and me."

3

ADAM felt very happy as he went home with his mother.

"First I thought I wouldn't like Mr John Miller," he told his mother, "but now I like him a lot. Then I thought I wouldn't like David, but I like him too. We had a lot of fun with that bus. It seems a long time, waiting until tomorrow. I didn't know the holidays would be so exciting."

Adam dreamed all night about the bus under the creeper. He dreamed he was inside it sitting in the driver's seat. In his dream the bus grew bare brown feet and ran down the road. Adam woke up suddenly. His mother was shaking him.

"Wake up!" she said. "It's breakfast time and you have got a visitor in the kitchen."

Adam got out of bed. He went into the kitchen and there was David.

"Hello," David said cheerfully. "I've been up for ages already. Mr Miller has to get up early to milk his cow. This morning, after he had milked his cow, he got all sorts of planks to finish the new floor in the bus."

"I'll have some breakfast first and then I'll come and help," said Adam.

"Perhaps David would like to have breakfast with you," suggested Adam's mother.

"I've had breakfast already," David said sadly.

Adam's mother laughed. "I think you will have room for some stewed apple, and perhaps you'd like some toast and honey too."

So David had two breakfasts. "It is a good idea to have two breakfasts," he told Adam. "It doesn't seem so long to wait until lunch time now. Get dressed and come down to Mr Miller's house. Put on your oldest clothes."

"Why?" asked Adam.

"It is a secret. Just put on your oldest clothes – that's all," said David, smiling sideways at the milk jug.

Outside it was a hot bright day. The sun was trying to be everywhere at once. The dust and stones on the road were already warm in the sunshine.

Mr John Miller was making bread. He had mixed up flour and water and sugar and some fizzy stuff called yeast. When the boys came into the kitchen Mr John Miller was putting butter inside his bread tins.

"If I don't put butter round the tins the bread sticks to them," he said. "Then I can't get the bread out of the tins."

"I thought you got bread from a shop," David said.

"I like to make my own bread," said Mr John Miller. "I like it better than shop bread. Now I mustn't forget that salt."

Mr John Miller only half filled the tins with the bread mixture.

"Why don't you fill the tins up to the top?" asked David.

"You'll see," Mr John Miller replied. "Now, I

will stand the tins by my old wood stove and put some pine cones on the fire. This bread must be kept warm you know. Then we'll go outside and have a look at that bus. I've nearly finished the floor for you."

There was the bus at the back of the dump. Mr John Miller had made a little path to it through the rusty machinery and tyres. Just where the lawn ended and the path began were a lot of tins standing in two rows.

"See!" cried David. "That's the secret. We're going to paint the bus."

The tins were all paint tins. Some had a little bit of paint left in them, but others were quite full.

"I had a look in my workshop," Mr John Miller said, "and I found all this old paint. You can use it up. I don't expect I'll need it again. We'll make a really bright bus of it by the time we're done. You boys can do the painting while I finish the floor. Only use one colour at a time, and be careful to clean your brushes in that pot there before you use another colour. There are lots of rags to wipe the brushes on."

Adam looked at the paints. There were seven of them and all of them different. There was a big pot with a lot of red paint in it. There was a pot with a little bit of yellow in the bottom. There was a dark blue pot, a bright green pot and one as pink as ice cream, looking as if it would be delicious to eat. The other two pots were dried up and no good at all. David took the red paint and Adam took the green. They began their painting one at each end of the bus. They painted carefully, trying not to waste any paint. But it was surprising how quickly the paint was used up. The green paint was finished first. Adam cleaned his brush and started on the pink paint. When he saw Adam starting on the pink paint, David grew tired of painting in red.

"There is too much red colour," he said. "I think I'll use the yellow now." He cleaned his brush and took the yellow paint.

When they came to a rusty patch they painted round it. If they tried to paint over it the rust came off and spoiled the colour.

Mr John Miller came out of the bus. "The floor is

finished boys, come and try it," he said. They went in to look at it. They found they could run from one end of the bus to the other because most of the seats were gone, and the floor was strong and clean. There was enough room to fight and dance and do a lot of things you could not do in a bus full of seats.

"It is going to be a wonderful fort," David cried. "It will be the best fort I have ever seen." He did not lookwhite-faced any more. He looked very red instead because he was so hot.

"You need a rest," said Mr John Miller. "Come and see how the bread is getting on, and we'll drink a glass of ginger-beer."

When they looked at the bread they were surprised to see it had risen up until the bread tins were full.

"It is the yeast that makes it do that," Mr John Miller told them. "Some people like it to rise twice, but I'm going to put it in the oven now. This is man's bread! Let's take the alarm clock into the garden. Then, when it goes off, we'll know it is time to take the bread out of the oven."

After they had drunk their ginger-beer they went back to painting. Adam had a turn with the red paint. David tried the blue. Their arms began to ache. Paint got splashed on their clothes and even in

their hair. They stood on boxes to reach up high. Soon there was nothing left except red paint, and there was only a little bit of that. Half of the door was painted yellow. They painted the other half red.

Now the bus was the brightest bus in the world. It was a patchwork bus – all colours. In one place the the red and blue paint had mixed together to make purple colour. In another place the blue and yellow had made a very dark green. Every now and then there was a patch of reddish, brownish rust.

"Gosh – it's really pretty," Adam said. "It's like a magic house but it has been hard work painting. Do you feel hot?" David was redder than ever.

"I'm very hot," he said. "I think Mr John Miller could bake his bread on me!"

Just then Mr John Miller's alarm clock went off with a sound like a fire engine. The boys ran inside to see him take the bread out of the oven. He lifted it out carefully. It was brown and crusty and smelt wonderful. Because it was too hot to eat they put it on the window-sill to cool. Then they went outside again.

"I've made up a riddle," said David. "What is the difference between Mr Miller's bread and the old bus?"

"I don't know," said Adam.

"Neither do I," sighed Mr John Miller. "Riddles are always too hard for me."

"Well," David replied, "the bread is brown and crusty and the bus is brown and rusty."

"The bus isn't brown any more," Adam said.

"It certainly isn't!" agreed Mr John Miller. "Now we must leave the paint to dry."

"We must leave the bread to cool," said David. "The bread and the bus must be left alone for a while."

All day David and Adam played together. The sun was hot. It began to dry the paint on the bus. At the end of the day David's arms and his legs and his back and his face were sunburnt.

"You're red as a fire," Adam said.

"I feel hot and sore," David told him. "But maybe I'll go brown like you. I didn't think I was going to like this holiday, but I'm glad I came."

As they came to Mr John Miller's house they touched the bus. Its paint was very nearly dry.

"Tomorrow we'll play in it all the time," said David. "We'll have lots of fun. It's been good today, painting the bus, but tomorrow will be even better."

"When I have had my tea," said Adam, "I am going to draw a picture with my coloured pencils. I am going to draw us painting the bus and Mr John Miller baking bread."

"I wish I'd brought my coloured pencils," said David, "or even some crayons."

Mr John Miller was sweeping his kitchen steps. "I have an old box of paints somewhere," he said. "You can have them. You've been painting all morning. Do you want to paint all night too?"

"Painting a picture is different from painting a bus," said David. "I'd like to paint a picture. Then I'd be able to show my picture to Adam tomorrow and he'd show me his."

"We will hang them in the bus," said Adam. "Then the bus will be full of colours inside as well as outside."

Then he went home to his mother, and Mr John Miller and David went in to eat scrambled eggs and slices of the fresh bread and honey.

4

ANOTHER fine day was beginning. The sun was shining on the hills and the fields. First it warmed the big pine trees and the little daisies. Then it looked in at Adam's window and woke him up. Beside his bed was the picture he had drawn the night before. It was a picture of David and Adam painting the old bus. David was drawn in a bright red colour because he was sunburnt.

The sun looked in at David's window too. It shone on the picture he had painted last night, which showed Adam and David pulling the creeper off the bus. It was full of gay colours.

After breakfast Adam took his picture down to show David. David was already inside the bus. He had a pot of paste and he was pasting his picture on the wall.

"Have you drawn a picture too?" Adam cried. "Look at the picture I drew last night. It is of you and me painting the bus. You are red because you are sunburnt."

David stared at the picture. He looked cross. "I wasn't as red as that," he said, "and now I am not red at all. Mr John Miller put sunburn oil on me and my sunburn stopped stinging. You have drawn me too red."

"I only had one pencil in my pencil box," Adam explained. "Your picture is a pretty one."

"It's a painted picture," said David. "Paints are much harder than pencils. Pencils stay in the same place but paints go everywhere. You paste your picture up beside mine. They'll look good to-gether."

They pasted Adam's picture up beside David's. The paste made the paper wrinkle up a little bit. They rubbed the wrinkles out with their sleeves.

While they were doing this Mr John Miller came into the bus.

"Well, what do you think!" he said. "We're having a visitor. Someone else is coming to play with you – a little girl called Anne."

"A girl," cried David. "We don't want any girl. This is our bus and it's only for boys."

Adam asked Mr John Miller, "Is it Anne Martin who goes to my school?"

"Yes," said Mr John Miller. "Her father asked if she could come and play this afternoon. She lives on a farm a long way off in the hills, and sometimes she gets lonely."

"I like Anne," said Adam. "You'll like her too, David. She can milk a cow and climb high trees. She is older than us though. She's eight."

"I don't care," David said sulkily. "I don't like girls and I don't want her in our bus. I won't talk to her."

Mr John Miller looked surprised. He blinked his eyes at David and scratched the back of his head.

"Dear me," he said. "I did not know girls were so difficult, or I wouldn't have asked her to come. It's too late now though. She is coming and you must be nice to her for today."

David did not say anything until Mr John Miller had gone. Then he looked at Adam with a frown all over his face.

"Now the day is spoilt," he cried. "If we have a girl here, we won't be able to play any good games." He sounded so cross that Adam didn't know what to say. He wanted to tell David that Anne would like playing pirates or bear hunting. She always liked exciting games. But Adam was sure that David would not believe him.

David looked at the bus wearing its new painted patchwork coat. He said to Adam, "I am going to make a real fort of this bus. You can help me. When the girl comes she can talk to Mr John Miller instead of us."

Adam watched while David searched around the scrap heap. He found two straight sticks. One was an old broom handle.

"These can be our guns," David cried. "This broom handle is a special gun. It can fire a hundred bullets – bang, bang, bang, bang – like that. If the girl tries to get into our bus I'll shoot her."

Adam liked the thought of having a gun. He forgot how much he liked Anne. He took up the other straight stick.

"This is my gun," he said. Then he swished it in the air and got another idea instead.

"It isn't really a gun," he told David. "This is a sword. I can cut through steel bars with it. If any enemy had an iron door I could cut it down."

"I could shoot it down," cried David quickly.

They looked around the scrap heap again. Adam found an old rusty bar with a wheel on it. He could turn the wheel round and round. They carried it into the bus and put it in the doorway. They pretended it was a big gun – a cannon. When they turned the handle the cannon went *boom* and shot down their enemies.

All morning they played that fierce cruel enemies were trying to get into the bus. They shot the enemies with the cannon, then chased them with the sword and the gun that shot a hundred bullets. Sometimes the enemies were all killed. Sometimes they came back to fight again.

Adam had to go home for lunch.

"Come back soon," David said, "so that we can both fight the girl." So Adam ran home, ate his lunch quickly and then ran back again.

The door of the bus was open, but the doorway was all filled up with armfuls of creeper piled on top of tree branches and sticks. David looked out of the window.

"There is a secret word to say before I let you in," he cried.

"I can't say it when I don't even know it," Adam called back.

David came down from the window and looked

through the tree branches at Adam. "The word is 'Blackbeetle'," he whispered. Then he pulled a branch away. Adam climbed through into the bus. He had to go in on his hands and knees.

"We will surprise that girl," said David.

"She is a nice girl really," Adam told him. David took no notice.

"Bang, bang, bang!" he shouted, firing his hundred-bullet gun at a bird.

Suddenly they heard a new sound – a funny clopping sound.

"What is it?" said David. "Is it someone walking in big shoes?"

"It's horses," Adam said. "Anne's coming, I think. She's got a horse called Pepper." He looked out of the window. "Yes, I can just see her coming round the side of the house. She is riding Pepper and leading another horse." He looked at David and David looked at him.

"You didn't tell me she would ride a horse," said David.

"I didn't know she'd bring it," said Adam. "She

rides her horse to school sometimes. She lets us ride
it."

David's eyes grew round.

"Does she?" he cried. "Would she let me ride it
do you think?"

"Of course," Adam said. "She is a nice girl."

Anne rode on to Mr John Miller's lawn with two
horses. Mr John Miller came out to meet her.

"Hello, Anne!" he said. "There are two boys
somewhere around. Have you seen them?"

"Hello, Mr Miller," said Anne. "I didn't see the

boys. I've brought an old horse called Nick in case they would like a ride."

David pushed Adam with his elbow.

"Let's go out," he said. "I think Anne might be a good sort of girl after all. Don't tell her I wanted to shoot at her will you? Do you think I will be able to ride on that horse by myself?"

Anne was pleased to see the boys. They took it in turns to ride the old horse Nick. David got so excited that his smooth black hair stuck up on end like a hedgehog's bristles. He got more and more sunburnt. Mr John Miller made him put on a big hat. When he rode round the paddock he looked like a mushroom riding a horse. It was very funny. He rode so well that Anne let him ride her own horse Pepper. David was delighted. "Anne is a good sort of girl," he said to Adam. "I told you she was. We must let her into the bus to play."

When it was tea time they cooked tea outside over a fire. They cooked sausages. Then they ate their tea sitting in the bus. Even Mr John Miller came into the bus to eat with them.

"What are the sticks in the windows for?" asked
Anne, staring at the gun that could fire a hundred
bullets.

David looked sternly at Adam. "They are just
sticks," he said. David did not want Anne to know
he had wanted to shoot at her and scare her away.

"Can you come again tomorrow?" he said.

"Not tomorrow!" Anne said. "They are cutting
down trees at our place – big tall pine trees. If I'm

not there they might cut down the tree with my swing on it. Why don't you come visiting me instead?"

"We will see tomorrow!" said Mr John Miller.

Then it was time for Anne to go home. They waved as she went down the road – clop, clop, riding her horse Pepper and leading her horse Nick.

"This is a wonderful day for me," David said to Adam. "I've not ridden a horse ever before and I have always wanted to. That Anne is a good sort of girl."

"I told you that," Adam said. David took no notice.

"I will do a drawing tonight," he said. "I will draw Anne and her horses, with me riding the horses. I'll draw Pepper trying to buck me off. I will be hanging on tightly though and not falling off at all. I'll paint it in all the brightest colours, and tomorrow we can hang it in the bus."

He grinned all over his face because he felt so happy.

5

It was a windy day. David woke up and heard the
north wind roaring in the trees. It sounded like a
hundred lions: it sounded like the sea. Adam came
running down the hill. The wind made his hair
stand on end. In his hand he held a new drawing.
The wind tried to pull it away from him.

Adam's picture and David's picture both showed
boys riding wild horses. They stuck them side by
side in the bus. Now there were four pictures.

Mr John Miller called them.

"Anne has just telephoned," he said. "She wants us to go and see the men cut down some big trees near her house. Would you like to go and watch?"

"Are they chopping them down with an axe?" asked David.

"No – they have a saw – a special saw called a chain-saw," said Mr John Miller. "We will get in my car and go and see them. The trees are very big. They are pine trees and they are seventy years old."

"Seventy years!" David said. "That is very old."

"Yes, it is," said Mr John Miller, "but it is not as old as I am. I am seventy-one."

Adam and David were surprised to think anyone could be as old as that.

They got into Mr John Miller's car and went over a windy road up into the hills. The higher they got the farther they could see. They could see the green roof of Adam's house. They could see the red roof of Mr John Miller's house. The pine trees and the poplar trees made green patches on the brown hills. The pine trees were dark and shadowy. Sometimes they looked black.

50

Anne opened the gate to let them in. She waved her straw hat. Mrs Martin, Anne's mother, stood at the door of the house.

"Hello, John," she said to Mr John Miller. "They are just going to cut down the first tree. Take the boys round to the back, Anne. You must show them where to stand."

The pine trees were in a row along the fence. The wind pushed and pulled them. It roared in their branches like a hundred lions. Men were talking and looking at the trees. David had never seen such tall trees. They had lots and lots of grey wrinkled branches, and all along the branches were pine cones.

The tree at the end of the row was the tallest of all. It had a swing tied to one of its branches.

"That is my swing," said Anne. "I hope they don't cut that tree down. It is a good swing."

Each pine tree had a trunk like a long strong leg. Each tree had big twisty roots like toes digging into the ground. David thought the trees looked like great giants with a hundred arms. Adam thought they looked like big green birds standing on one leg with the other leg curled up out of sight.

Adam said to David, "Suppose that they started to saw the trees down and all the trees put down another leg. Suppose all the trees ran away over the hill."

David did not know what Adam was talking about.

There was a thick rope. One end was tied to a tree. The other end was fastened to a machine on the back of a truck. The machine was called a winch. It pulled the ropes tightly.

"All right – off we go!" said one of the men. He picked up the chain-saw. The chain-saw had a little motor on it. When the man switched it on the saw made an angry screaming noise. First the man cut a piece out of one side of the tree trunk. Then he went round to the other side of the tree.

"Scream! Scream!" went the chain-saw. Then the man stopped sawing the tree.

"All right – give it a go!" he shouted. The truck engine started up. The winch wound the rope and pulled it tightly. The rope began to pull the tree. David and Adam stared. At first it seemed as if nothing was going to happen; then there was a cracking, creaking sound and the tree started to lean over to one side. It fell very slowly at first. Then suddenly it fell quickly. There was a crash like thunder as it fell. Branches broke. Pine cones flew into the air like brown birds.

"I felt afraid," said David. "I thought it would fall on top of us."

"It looked as if it was scratching the sky down," Adam cried.

"Didn't it bang and crash?" yelled Anne. "Listen to the hens."

The hens were clucking and squawking. They were frightened too.

"Now the men are going to cut down another tree," Anne said.

David, Adam, Anne and Mr John Miller watched the men cut down three more trees. The ground felt shaky when the trees fell.

"Just think," said Mr John Miller, "these trees

have been growing a long time. They grew from seeds smaller than my finger nail. It took seventy years for them to grow so tall and to grow all those branches and pine cones. Now someone has cut them down. It's only taken ten minutes to cut them down."

"They are stopping," David said. "Anne's mother is bringing out some cakes."

"We'll have some too," said Anne. "There are lots of cakes."

Anne's mother gave them a cake each. They went to look at the fallen trees. They climbed in and out of the branches. They sniffed the pine-tree smell. On their hands and knees were brown stains from pine-tree gum. There were lots of prickly green cones under the pine needles. Each tree was like a house full of rooms and passages.

"We could get pillows and live here," David said. "It would be fun to sleep in a pine tree."

"We could see the stars at night looking in between the branches," said Adam.

Then the men shouted to them. They were going

to cut down more trees. The children got out of the way. Soon the chain-saw was screaming again and another great pine tree fell to the ground.

"It is a bit sad," said Adam, "to see those old trees cut down. They are nice trees."

"It is exciting when they go BANG though!" David said. "I like that."

"I like it when they fall," Adam said, "but I feel sorry afterwards."

At last there was only one tree left. It was the tree with Anne's swing on it.

"They are going to cut down my swing tree!" cried Anne. She looked very sad.

But the men did not cut it down. They began to pack up their chain-saw and ropes.

"Aren't you going to cut down that tree?" David asked.

"No!" said one of the men. "It is a fine old tree. It is still strong and green. We will leave it to grow for another seventy years."

"Hooray!" Anne shouted. "My swing is safe. I can go high on that swing. Come and try it."

The boys ran to try the swing before they went home. It was a wonderful swing with long ropes. Adam stood up with his feet on the flat wooden swing-seat. He swung high. When he looked up he could see blue sky through the branches. He could see sunlight on the pine cones. "I am glad they kept this old pine tree," he thought. "I think Mr John Miller is glad too."

As they rode home in Mr John Miller's car Adam asked him if he was glad that the last old pine tree had not been cut down.

"Yes, I am pleased," said Mr John Miller. "I know some old trees must be cut down, but I like trees. I think they are very grand and beautiful. Some trees are more than a hundred years old."

"More than five hundred?" asked David. Mr John Miller laughed.

"Some trees are a thousand years old," he said.

"It would have made a big crash if they had cut down that last old tree," David said. "It was the biggest tree of all."

"Tonight you can paint a picture of the trees,"

Mr John Miller told him. "You will be able to paint the trees falling down. They will make a grand picture."

"Yes!" David said. "I hope I don't run out of green paint. I will need a lot."

"You'll have lots of pictures in the old bus by the end of the holidays," said Mr John Miller.

His car went bump bump down the road as they went home over the brown hills. The wind ran beside them roaring like a hundred lions.

6

THE days of the holiday were all sunny and warm.
Every morning when Adam woke up and looked
outside the sky was blue and the sun was shining.
Adam thought the holiday would go on forever. He
forgot that David would have to go back home.
They had such a lot of adventures together, chasing
eels, building dams over the creek, swimming and
just running around. They rattled down the hill in
the blue trolley tooting cheerfully as they went.
Inside, the bus was covered with pictures. It looked
very bright and gay. There were two pictures for
every day of the holidays – one picture of David's

and one picture of Adam's. Mr John Miller had put a shelf in the bus. On it stood a big jar of tadpoles which the boys had caught. In another corner was an eel spear and two fishing lines.

And then suddenly the holiday was over and it was time for David to go home. David and Adam and Mr John Miller sat on the lawn drinking ginger-beer sadly. They didn't want to say good-bye to one another.

"Tomorrow afternoon," David said, "my father is coming to get me in our green car. You'll like our car, Adam. It is faster than lightning."

"Are you glad to be going home?" asked Adam.

"I am a bit glad and a bit sorry," David said. "I wish you could come too. I'd like to take the bus home with me – and the creek too, and the eels and Anne and her horses."

"You'd have a very heavy suitcase," said Adam. He felt sad.

"I'll miss you David," he said.

"I will miss you both," said Mr John Miller. "David will be gone home, and Adam will be at school. Who'll play in the bus? Who will drink ginger-beer with me?"

"I'll come and see you after school," Adam told him.

Suddenly Mr John Miller smiled. "We are getting a bit too sad," he said. "I have an idea to make us happy again. We'll have a party tomorrow when David's father and mother come to collect him. Yes – we will have an outside party. This afternoon I'll bake some cakes. Then tomorrow we'll light a fire outside and cook sausages over it. Adam's mother and father will be invited, and we'll ask Anne's mother if Anne can come too. Is that a good idea?"

"Yes! Yes!" shouted David and Adam. They had something to look forward to now. They did not feel nearly so sad.

Mr John Miller spent most of the afternoon baking cakes. The kitchen was full of wonderful smells. It smelt of sugar, raisins, and cakes in the oven. David and Adam helped him. They beat the eggs until they were frothy. They licked the spoons and scraped the bowls. "How lucky I am to have two such good helpers," said Mr John Miller. "Usually I have to scrape the bowls myself. I get very tired of scraping bowls."

"I could scrape a million bowls," said David. "Or ten anyway."

Mr John Miller baked three big cakes and a lot of little ones. He did not have a cook book. "I put in a spoonful of this, a cupful of that, and two handfuls of raisins and currants and things," said Mr John Miller. The little cakes were in paper patty pans. Some were pink, some were yellow, some were blue. They looked very pretty.

"I will ice the big cakes tonight," said Mr John Miller, "and make some toffee too."

That night, just before he went to bed, Adam looked out of the door of his own kitchen. Below him, across the road and down the hill, he could see a light in Mr John Miller's kitchen. Mr John Miller was icing the cakes.

Adam thought Mr John Miller was a jolly good sort. He said to his mother, "Are you looking forward to the party tomorrow?"

"Yes, I'm feeling very excited. It's a long time since I have been to a party," said his mother.

"It isn't long to wait now!" said Adam happily, as he went to bed.

You should have seen Mr John Miller's garden next afternoon. Adam and David and Mr John Miller were there of course. There was Anne wearing a pink frock. There was Adam's mother and his father too. David stood first on one foot and then on the other. He was very excited at the thought of seeing his mother and father again.

"Have I grown?" he asked. "Am I taller? I am quite brown now I know."

Adam looked at David.

"Yes," he said. "You used to have a white face, but now it is brown. Your legs are brown too and your nose has got freckles. Your hair sticks up in the air and you are a bit fatter. Your mother will wonder who you are."

Toot! Toot! What was that? It was a car coming in at Mr John Miller's gate – a long green car with four headlights. It was Mr and Mrs Ryan, David's father and mother.

"Is that David?" cried his mother.

"What a brown fellow we have now," said his father. "He looks as if he could fight a bear."

"I could fight a hundred bears," said David and gave his mother a big bear hug.

When everyone had said Hello to everyone else David shouted, "Come and see our bus! Adam, we must show them the bus."

"I must see the bus," said Adam's father. "Adam

has told me all about it. Now I'll just have to see it for myself."

They went round to the back of Mr John Miller's house. There was the bus in the old dump. The green creeper was growing all over its roof. Its windows looked out like a lot of eyes peeping under green hair. Its door was like a funny little surprised mouth at one side of its face. There were certainly a lot of colours on that bus.

"It looks like a sunset," said Adam's mother.

"Or like a bed of flowers," said David's mother.

"It looks like a funny bright-coloured caterpillar," said Anne. "Inside it is full of pictures. Let's go in and see them."

David, Adam and Mr John Miller invited the mothers and fathers and Anne into the bus. All the walls were covered with the holiday pictures.

"Look, Mum," said David, "these are the first pictures we drew. See how Adam drew me all red? I was very sunburnt. That was the day we painted the bus."

"Look," Adam said. "This is David and me riding

Anne's horses. David wore a big sunhat – he looked like a mushroom on a horse."

"This is the day they came to our place," Anne said, pointing.

"These are the pine trees falling over. They look as if they are falling on us, but they didn't really."

There were pictures of David and Adam catching eels as big as sea serpents. There were pictures of David and Adam making high dams out of stones and swimming in deep water. There were pictures of camp fires, and cooking sausages outside. There were pictures of Mr John Miller making bread and milking his cow. The mothers and fathers looked at all the pictures. They liked them all so much they could not say which one they liked best. "I can see you've had a wonderful holiday, David," said Mr Ryan.

"It was the nicest holiday I have ever had," said David, "and it isn't over yet. We're going to have a party."

Mr John Miller found an old door in his workshop. He laid it on two boxes. This made a table on the lawn. He covered it with an old blue curtain. The fathers made a fireplace out of bricks on the edge of the dump. The fire burned merrily. Then the party began. Everyone had sausages to cook over the fire. They stood round the fire laughing and talking. David's sausage fell into the fire twice. His father got it out with a pointed stick. The whole garden smelt of cooking sausage.

"Mr John Miller makes his own bread," David said to his father. "It is the best bread in the world."

Then Mr John Miller went into the house and made a big pot of tea. David and Adam helped him carry out the cups, the sugar and the milk. Then they went back for the cakes. Out came plates of little cakes in pretty paper patty pans. Out came a brown chocolate cake covered with hundreds and thousands. Last of all Mr John Miller carried out a big tea tray with a tea towel over it. No one could see what was on it.

"Do you know what it is?" whispered Adam to David. "No," whispered David. "It must be a surprise."

Mr John Miller heard him.

"It is a surprise," he said. "I hope you like it."
Then he pulled off the tea towel.

There were the two biggest cakes. They were
covered in white icing. Each had a name on it. One
had "Adam" written on it in pink icing. The other
cake had "David". David and Adam were very
pleased.

"A whole cake each!" cried David. "Shall we eat every bit ourselves?"

"No!" said Adam's mother and David's mother quickly.

"No!" said Mr John Miller, "but you can each have a big slice and then I will wrap the cakes up and you can take them home."

Everyone had tea and cakes and laughed and talked some more.

Then it was time for David to go home. He went with his father to get his suitcase. Adam tried to look as if he didn't care but he felt all sorry inside. David's mother said to him, "Don't look so sad, Adam. We will bring David to see you again very soon. We will come out one Saturday. You'll hear the car tooting and there we will be; then, when it is holiday time again, David will come and stay with Mr John Miller. You will be able to have more adventures."

"And I'll come," said Anne. "I'll bring my horses too."

"So you see David is not going away forever,"

said David's mother. "The good times are just be-ginning, not coming to an end."

David came out carrying his suitcase. He had one last look in the bus.

"I am coming back next holidays," he said to Adam. "We'll draw a lot more pictures. We've had a good holiday in that old bus, haven't we Adam?"

"We've had the best holiday in the world," said Adam.

Then David got into the green car. His father started the car up and they drove out of the gate. Adam waved. Anne waved. Mr John Miller waved. "Good-bye," they called. "Good-bye David. Come again soon."

Yes, it was good-bye until next holidays – good-bye to the brightly-coloured bus, the poplar trees, the creek, the brown paddocks, and the valley be-tween the hills.

MORE ABOUT PENGUINS

For further information about books available from Penguin please write to the following:

In New Zealand: For a complete list of books available from Penguin in New Zealand write to the Marketing Department, Penguin Books (N.Z.) Ltd, Private Bag, Takapuna, Auckland.

In Australia: For a complete list of books available from Penguin in Australia write to the Marketing Department, Penguin Books Australia Ltd, P.O. Box 257, Ringwood, Victoria 3134.

In Britain: For a complete list of books available from Penguin in Britain write to Dept EP, Penguin Books Ltd, Harmondsworth, Middlesex UB7 0DA.

In the U.S.A.: For a complete list of books available from Penguin in the United States write to Dept DG, Penguin Books, 299 Murray Hill Parkway, East Rutherford, New Jersey 07073.

In Canada: For a complete list of books available from Penguin in Canada write to Penguin Books Canada Ltd, 2801 John Street, Markham, Ontario L3R 1B4.

Margaret Mahy in Puffins

CLANCY'S CABIN

'Turn the world over and if you're not blind,
The way to the treasure you're certain to find . . .'

Clancy's cabin is a wonderful place for Skip, Timothy and Marina to spend a camping holiday.

It is high summer, when the days are blue and warm, ideal for swimming, for camp fires and adventuring – and for treasure hunting.

When the children find a clue to hidden treasure they think at first that their father has hidden it for them to find. After all, he's always playing jokes on them. But *is* it a joke this time?

A Young Puffin

THE PIRATE UNCLE

'I *was* a pirate. Now I'm trying to give it up, and I need help.'

Uncle Ludovic has a great black beard hanging down his chest like a doormat. He claims to be a pirate trying to mend his ways.

One summer Caroline and Nicholas spend a wonderful holiday with him – there's breakfast on the beach, swimming and sailing, and treasure hunting in the house when it rains.

Sometimes Uncle Ludovic certainly does some very piratical things. But soon Caroline hits on a sure way to reform their pirate uncle.

An intriguing tale which boys and girls of a wide age range will enjoy.

A Young Puffin